In loving memory of Dory
Hey, don't ever hide your love away.

First published in Belgium and Holland by Clavis Uitgeverij, Hasselt – Amsterdam, 2015
Copyright © 2015, Clavis Uitgeverij

English translation from the Dutch by Clavis Publishing Inc. New York
Copyright © 2016 for the English language edition: Clavis Publishing Inc. New York

Visit us on the web at www.clavisbooks.com

Everywhere and All Around written by Pimm van Hest and illustrated by Sassafras De Bruyn
Original title: *Overal en ergens*
Translated from the Dutch by Clavis Publishing

ISBN 978-1-60537-269-3

This book was printed in April 2016 at Publikum d.o.o., Slavka Rodica 6, Belgrade, Serbia

First Edition
10 9 8 7 6 5 4 3 2 1

Pimm van Hest
Sassafras De Bruyn

Everywhere
and all around

Clavis

NEW YORK

Yolanda's mom has died.
Passed away. Gone.

Yolanda misses her very much.
So much… there are no words to describe how much.

One moment, Yolanda had been able to talk with her.
The next, she stopped breathing. Her heart stood still.
Yolanda stayed with her for a very long time, holding her hand….
It slowly grew cold.
Her mom was still there, and yet she wasn't.

People don't like to talk about death.
They'd rather be quiet. Quiet like her Mom is now.
Yolanda doesn't want to be quiet.
She wants to know where her mom is.
She has to be somewhere, right?

"If you look for me, my darling, you will find me."

So Yolanda decides to go looking.
Looking for her mom.
Her mom who has died.

She starts with Julian.
Her four-year-old brother.
Maybe he knows where Mom is.
His bedroom door is ajar.
She hears him talking.
Talking to Mom.
How is that possible?
Yolanda swings the door open.
Julian is sitting cross-legged on his bed.
Across from him is Bear.
Julian is talking to Bear.

Mom is Bear and Bear is Mom.

Yolanda goes back downstairs.
Dad is sitting at the table drinking a cup of coffee.
Yolanda sits down too.
"Dad, where do you think Mom is now?"
"Well…" he says.
There is a moment of silence.
Then he takes her photograph and puts it on the table.
"This is where Mom is to me now. Between us. On the table.
But she is also in this picture that she painted.
And in this mug that she glued back together.
And in the chair she always sat in, and in her coat
that is still hanging on the coat rack."

Mom is in things and in things is mom.

That evening in bed Yolanda thinks
about Julian and Dad.
She takes Bunny. Her cuddly toy.
Mom made Bunny for her.
Yolanda hugs Bunny firmly.
It feels nice.
Yolanda smells Bunny.
Bunny smells like Bunny.
And Bunny smells like Yolanda.
But Bunny also smells like Mom.
He has Mom's smell.
Suddenly Mom feels very close.
When she closes her eyes,
it's like Mom is cuddling her.

Mom is Bunny and Bunny is Mom.

The next day Aunt Christina drops by.
Mom's sister.
"Aunt Christina, do you know where Mom is now?"
Suddenly there are tears.
Yolanda is startled.
"These are tears of joy, sweetheart.
It is heartwarming to me that you ask about your mom.
As long as we talk about her, she is still with us.
If we stop talking about her and never think about her anymore,
then Mom will really be gone."
The rest of the afternoon Aunt Christina shares stories about Mom.
It's as if Mom is there with them.

Mom is in stories and in stories is Mom.

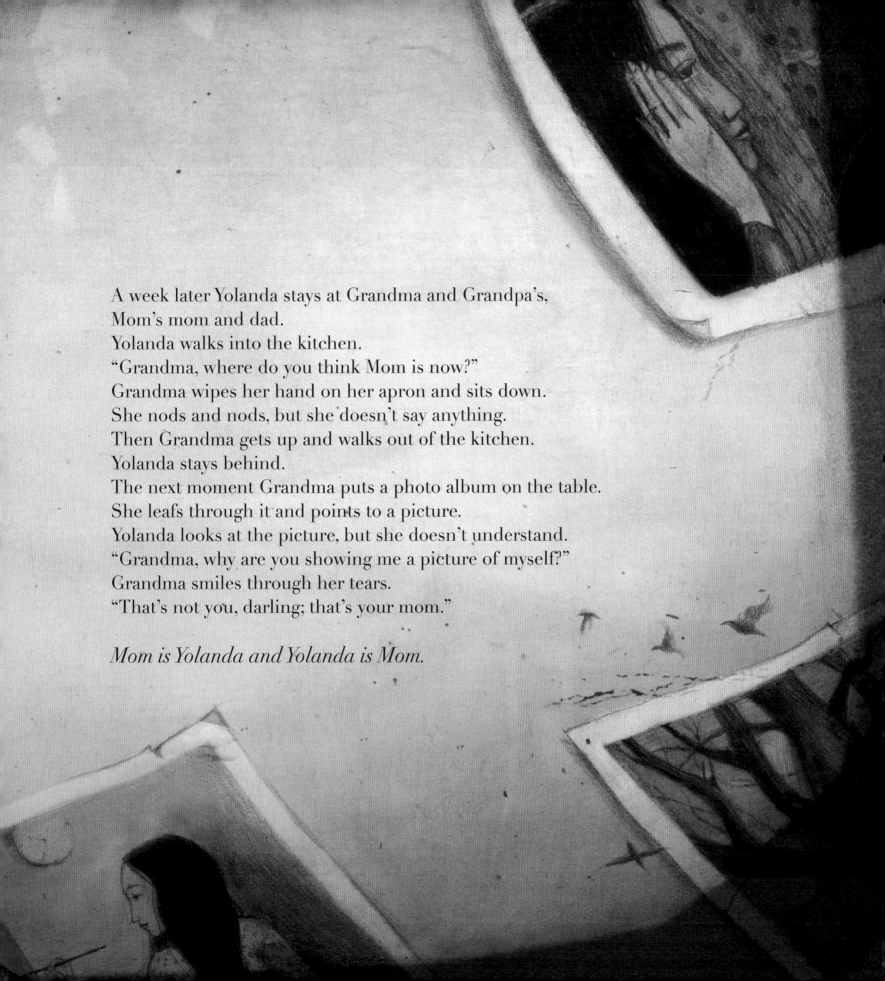

A week later Yolanda stays at Grandma and Grandpa's,
Mom's mom and dad.
Yolanda walks into the kitchen.
"Grandma, where do you think Mom is now?"
Grandma wipes her hand on her apron and sits down.
She nods and nods, but she doesn't say anything.
Then Grandma gets up and walks out of the kitchen.
Yolanda stays behind.
The next moment Grandma puts a photo album on the table.
She leafs through it and points to a picture.
Yolanda looks at the picture, but she doesn't understand.
"Grandma, why are you showing me a picture of myself?"
Grandma smiles through her tears.
"That's not you, darling; that's your mom."

Mom is Yolanda and Yolanda is Mom.

Yolanda goes to the cemetery with Grandpa.
He likes taking care of Mom's grave.
"Grandpa, where do you think Mom is now?"
Grandpa puts his rake down and sits on the grass.
"There is earth underneath this grass," Grandpa says,
"and Mom is buried in that earth.
Slowly but surely she will become earth again.
In spring grass and flowers will grow from that earth.
To me it will be like seeing your Mom again.
In some way she'll come back to life
in a flower, in a little worm that sticks its head out
from under the ground,
or in a delicious apple growing on the tree."

Mom is nature and nature is Mom.

Back at their house,
Grandpa takes Yolanda to a corner of the garden.
"Look, honey, the roses that grow over there
were planted by your mom when she was about your age.
Every year they bloom. Even now, after she's gone.
That's another way that Mom lives on."
Carefully, Grandpa snips off the prettiest rose and hands it to Yolanda.
"Put it in a vase next to your bed.
Then Mom will be very close."

Mom is the rose and the rose is Mom.

The next day the alarm clock rings early.
Willa, Mom's best friend, is taking Yolanda to the beach.
"To me your mom is here," Willa says as they walk by the ocean.
"Where?" Yolanda asks.
"In the wind. You can't see the wind, but you can feel it.
It's the same with your mom.
You can't see her, but she's still here.
Spread your arms, my love, close your eyes, and think about Mom.
Then you'll feel her."
For a moment Yolanda forgets everything.
Then she feels Mom's arms embracing her.
It makes Yolanda feel warm inside.

Mom is the wind and the wind is Mom.

When she goes to bed, Yolanda lies awake for a while.
Suddenly she remembers her teacher's words.
"I think your mom is now a beautiful star in the sky.
A little star that shines at night when you sleep and watches over you.
Your little light in the dark.
When you miss your mom, look up at the night sky.
You might see her somewhere among all those other stars."
Yolanda opens the curtains and looks up.
Even though Mom is very far away, at this moment she feels very close by.

Mom is a star and a star is Mom.

That night Yolanda has a beautiful dream.
She is sitting alone on a bench.
And Mom comes and sits next to her.
Just like that. Like she used to do.
"Hey," Yolanda says, "there you are.
I've been looking *everywhere* for you."
Mom leans closer and gives her a kiss.
"That's exactly where I am, my darling."

When Dad wakes her with a kiss the next morning,
Yolanda says: "I know where Mom is now."
"Where?" Dad asks.

"Mom is everywhere!"